Dedicated to all my former students in India, Canada, Brazil, and Mozambique from whom I learned.

Works Used

Period/Name	Time	Internet Reference
Neogene		
Scene	2013	http://upload.wikimedia.org/wikipedia/commons/5/53/Miocene.jpg
Palaeogene		
Scene	2011	http://upload.wikimedia.org/wikipedia/commons/3/3c/Eocene.jpg
Cretaceous		
Pterodactyl	2013	http://upload.wikimedia.org/wikipedia/commons/c/c9/Coloborhynchus_piscator_jconway.jpg
Tyrannosaurus	2007	Nobu Tamura http://spinopsblogspot.com http://upload.wikimedia.org/wikipedia/commons/a/a3/Tyrannaosaurus.BW.jpg
Tylosaurus	2007	Dmitry Bogdanov http://en.wikipedia.org/wiki/FileTyloraurusDB:jpg http://upload.wikimedia.org/wikipedia/commons/4/42/TylosaurusDB2.jpg
Jurassic		
Conifers	2008	http://upload.wikimedia.org/wikipedia/commons/6/66/Douglas_fir_leaves_and_bud.jpg
Diplodocus	2010	Nobu Tamura http://spinopsblogspot.com http://upload.wikimedia.org/wikipedia/commons/a/aa/Diplodocus_BW.jpg
Muraenosaurus	2008	http://en.wikipedia.org/wiki/FileMuraenosaurusDB:jpg (Dmitry Bogdanov) http://upload.wikimedia.org/wikipedia/commons/7/70/Muraenosaurus_12.jpg
Triassic		
Plateosaurus	2009	Nobu Tamura http://spinopsblogspot.com http://upload.wikimedia.org/wikipedia/commons/9/99/Sellosaurus.jpg
Sillisaurus Coelophysis	2006	http://upload.wikimedia.org/wikipedia/commons/1/1a/Coelophysis_Animatronics_model_NHM2.jpg
Cynognathus	2013	Nobu Tamura http://spinopsblogspot.com http://upload.wikimedia.org/wikipedia/commons/f/fd/Cynognathus_BW.jpg
Proterosuchus	2007	Nobu Tamura http://spinops.blogspot.com http://upload.wikimedia.org/wikipedia/commons/c/c9/Proterosuchus_BW.jpg
Lystrosaurus	2007	Nobu Tamura http://spinopsblogspot.com http://upload.wikimedia.org/wikipedia/commons/1/17/Lystrosaurus_BW.jpg
Permian		
Edaphosaurus Pogonius	2007	http://en.wikipedia.org/wiki/FileEdaphosaurusDB:jpg (Dmitry Bogdanov) http://upload.wikimedia.org/wikipedia/commons/b/b6/EdaphosaurusDB.jpg
Carboniferous		
Forest	1885-1890	http://en.wikipedia.org/wiki/FileMeyers_b15_s0272b.jpg
Pederpes	2007	DiBgdat en.wikipedia,dmitrchel@mail.ru ((Dmitry Bogdanov) http://en.wikipedia.org/w/index.php?title=ImagePederpes22small.jpg
Holynomus	2007	Nobu Tamura http://spinopsblogspot.com http://upload.wikimedia.org/wikipedia/commons/5/56/Hylonomus_BW.jpg
Devonian		
Forest	2013	http://en.wikipedia.org/wiki/File:Devonianscene-green.jpg
Silurian		
Fishes	2013	http://en.wikipedia.org/wiki/File:Silurianfishes_ntm_1905_smit_1929.gif
Cooksonis	2008	http://en. wikipedia.org/wiki/File:Cooksonia.png
Ordovician		
Graptolites	2008	http://upload.wikimedia.org/wikipedia/commons/d/dd/DiplograptusCarneySprings.jpg
Cambrian		
Trilobites	2011	http://upload.wikimedia.org/wikipedia/commons/8/8d/Trilobitegrowth.jpg

Special Thanks

I thank the palaeontologists and the organizations who have meticulously reconstructed the shapes of the species from the excavated bones over the past 150 years. Particularly let me mention the names Jay Matternes, Arthur Weasley, Nobu Tamura, SMITHSONIAN, WIKIPEDIA COMMONS, Uther SRG, Dmitry Bogdanov, Funk Monk, Frisfron, Joseph Smit 1836-1929, Wilson4469, vanhin tunnettu putkilokasvi. Kuva: Ville Koistinen, Finnish Wikipedia fi:Kuva:Cooksonia.png, and John Alan Elson. By no means is this list complete. To all those unknown and unmentioned in scientific reports and papers, we all owe a tremendous amount of gratitude. I thank Rosemarie for drawing excellent illustrations, Laura my editor, Maria my media editor, and Naren my publisher for making this project possible. Special thanks are due to Anne the fifth grader for special input.

www.mascotbooks.com

Life On Earth As Told by Owl

For more information, please contact:
Mascot Books
560 Herndon Parkway #120
Herndon, VA 20170
info@mascotbooks.com

Library of Congress Control Number: 2015904098

CPSIA Code: PRT1115A
ISBN-13: 978-1-62086-862-1

Printed in the United States

LIFE ON EARTH

As Told by Owl

Naveen Chandra Ph.D.

illustrated by Rosemarie Gillen

technical images designed by author

A bear cub was wandering along and saw a gosling. "I was wondering how life developed on Earth," said the cub.

"We should ask Mr. Owl." They both went to Owl.

"What brings you here?" asked Owl.

"Can you explain to us how life developed?" asked the bear cub.

"Okay!" Owl replied. "Do you remember how old the Earth is?" Owl was testing them.

They both said, "About 4.6 billion years old."

"That will do. I will teach you what my grandma taught me. First, there was the inanimate world of rocks, soil, water, ice, and air from which came flora and fauna. Life developed from simpler forms to more complex forms, from single cell to multi-cell organisms, from microorganisms that can only be seen under a microscope to macro-organisms seen with the naked eye, from invertebrates to vertebrates."

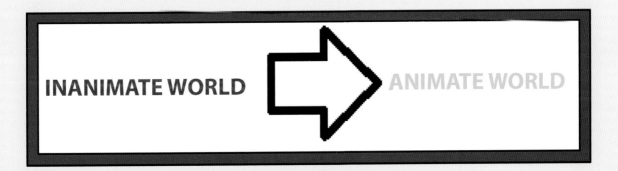

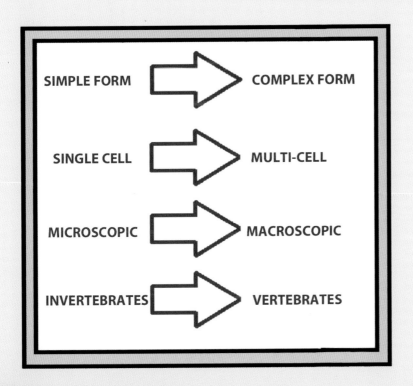

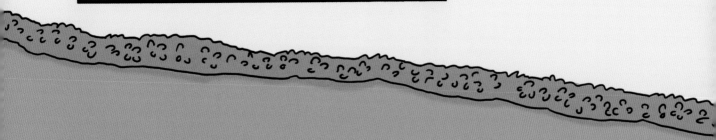

"What kind of evidence is used to know about life?" inquired the gosling.

"The organisms living in the seas died when the rocks were uplifted and the seas dried out. Later when the land subsided, new seas were formed, new rock layers were deposited, and the embedded, dead organisms became fossils. Geochronology helped date the rock layers which helped date the fossils themselves. Just like a year is divided into months, weeks, etc., the geological history is divided into eons, eras, etc. A million years ago is briefly denoted by 1 ma. The youngest fossil known is 10,000 years old and the oldest is 3.4 billion years old. Each time an old form died never to return, a new form of life better suited to new conditions emerged."

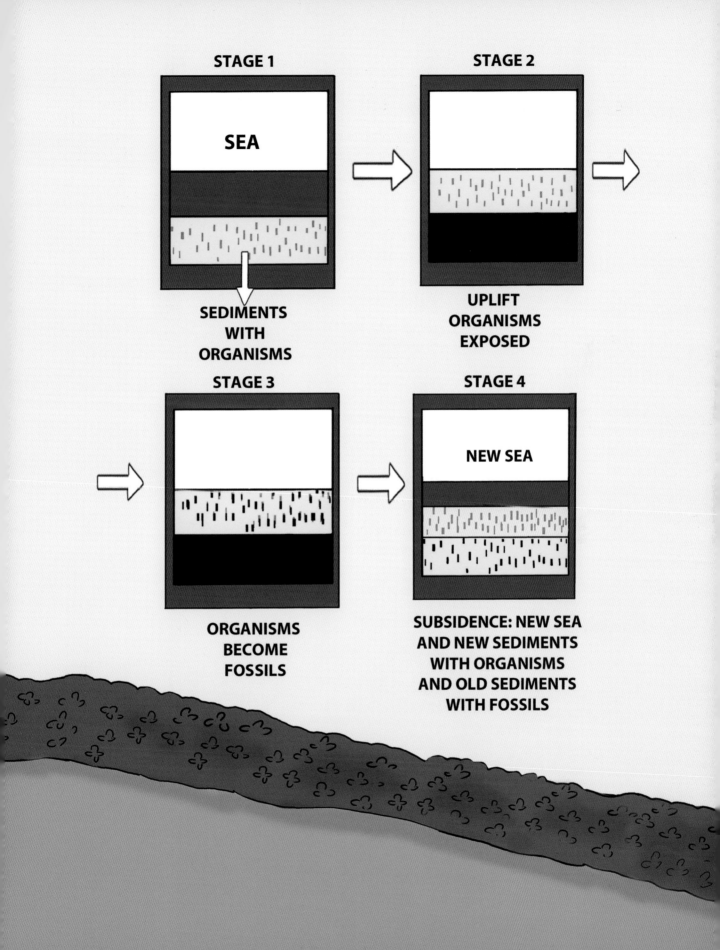

"What factors affected the seas, rocks, and organisms?" asked the cub.

"Life was fragile." Owl adjusted his glasses. "The earthquakes shook the earth, volcanoes erupted, rivers flowed, glaciers crawled, seas roared, winds blew, radiation from space flooded the earth, and meteorites hit in the past as they are doing today. Rivers carried sediment and deposited it in the seas giving rise to sedimentary rocks. Volcanoes produced volcanic rocks. Magma crystallized to form plutonic rocks. These rocks became metamorphic rocks under high pressures and high temperatures. Only sedimentary rocks preserved fossils as in other rocks high temperatures and pressures destroyed any life."

"So we did not exist then?" was the next question from the gosling.

"No. You will be surprised to know that 99.99% of organisms are extinct now. The five major extinctions of life are dated at 439 ma, at 364 ma, the worst at 251 ma, at 199-214 ma, and finally at 65 ma. There were other minor extinctions as well."

"Are there no old life forms alive today?"

"Not many. The algae and fungi of the remote past are still present today. So are some fish," said Owl.

"What are the names given to geological strata?"

"The younger Phanerozoic (visible life) Eon separated from the older Eons (Hadean, Archaen and Proterozoic) by the 600 ma reference datum is divided into Palaeozoic Era (Old Life 250-600 ma), Mesozoic Era (Middle Life 60-250 ma) and Cenozoic Era (Recent Life 2.5-60 ma). We are living in Quaternary Period that started 2.5 ma."

"Tell us about the three eras and what they mean," requested the cub.

"The Palaeozoic Era is divided into Cambrian, Ordovician, Silurian, Devonian, Carboniferous, and Permian Periods. The Mesozoic Era is divided into Triassic, Jurassic and Cretaceous. The Cenozoic is divided into Palaeogene and Neogene. The base of Palaeozoic Era is characterized by the explosion of Trilobites and other marine animals, the base of Mesozoic Era is characterized by their extinction, and the base of Cenozoic Era is characterized by the extinction of the dinosaurs."

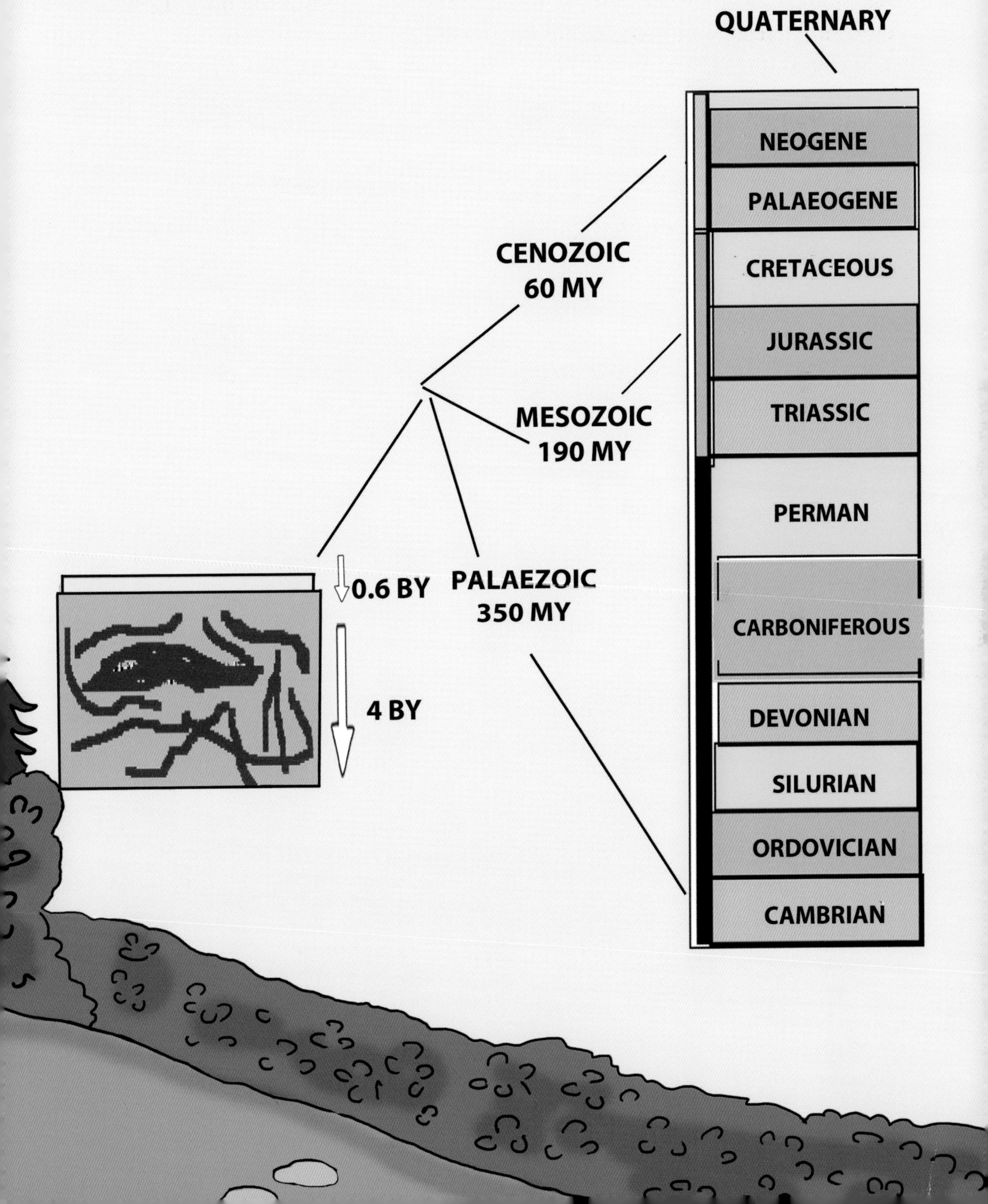

QUATERNARY

NEOGENE

PALAEOGENE

CRETACEOUS

JURASSIC

TRIASSIC

PERMAN

CARBONIFEROUS

DEVONIAN

SILURIAN

ORDOVICIAN

CAMBRIAN

CENOZOIC
60 MY

MESOZOIC
190 MY

0.6 BY

4 BY

PALAEZOIC
350 MY

"Tell us then what life forms existed in these remote geological periods," begged the gosling.

Owl began. "Marine invertebrate organisms, like Trilobites, that roamed the Cambrian seas became extinct as the beds were uplifted and the sea dried up. They are now just fossils in the rock stratum."

The little animals were listening closely, so Owl continued. "The Ordovician Period is noted for Graptolites and the first vertebrate fish. It is also marked by a major extinction of several marine organisms. The Ice Age, a gamma ray burst, weathering, and volcanoes are some of the reasons given for this extinction."

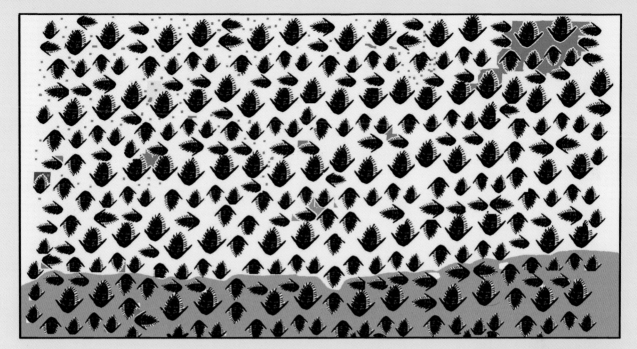

TRILOBITES

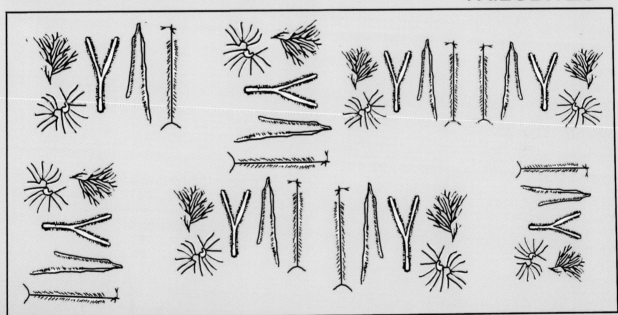

GRAPTOLITES

Owl pointed to the creek nearby. "In the Silurian Period, the first land flora formed moss forests along lakes and creeks like this one. The first fossil records of vascular plants, or land plants with tissues that carry food, appeared in the second half of the Silurian Period. The first bony fish appeared with bony scales and fish reached considerable diversity, developing movable jaws adapted from the supports of the front gill arches."

"The appearance of bark-bearing trees and the predominance of shallow seas made the extensive coal beds possible. In the Devonian, the seas were deeper. Cordaites fossils are found in rock sections from 323 to 299 ma. A cordaites is a tall plant (6 to 30 meters) with strap-like leaves, similar to palm trees."

SILURIAN FAUNA AND FLORA

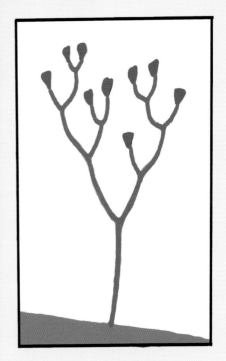

DEVONIAN FLORA

"In the Permian Period, ancestors of the mammals, turtles, and other reptiles came on the scene. There was only one supercontinent called Pangaea surrounded by a global ocean, Panthalassa. The forests of the Carboniferous period disappeared, leaving a large desert in the middle of the continent. Reptiles became more wide-spread at the expense of the amphibians. The Permian Period (and the Paleozoic Era) terminated in a mass extinction destroying 90-percent of marine species and 70-percent of terrestrial species." Owl looked a bit sad at this description of the extinction.

Owl continued as the little animals listened intently. "Terrestrial life was well established by the Carboniferous Period. Amphibians, the dominant land vertebrates, were precursors of reptiles. A minor marine and terrestrial extinction occurred in the middle of the period, caused by a change in climate. The latter half of the period experienced glaciations, low sea levels, and mountain building as the continents collided to form Pangaea."

"I remember Pangaea from the last story you told!" the cub exclaimed.

Owl was proud. "Very good. Now, to continue with this story."

CARBONIFEROUS
A FOUR LEGGED AMPHIBIAN

CARBONIFEROUS AN EARLY REPTILE

EARLY PERMIAN REPTILE

CARBONIFEROUS FOREST

"What came next?" the gosling asked.

"The Triassic Period came and saw both at its beginning and end a massive extinction of life forms. The first dinosaurs, mammals, and flying vertebrates appeared in this time. Pangaea gradually drifted into Laurasia and Gondwana in the middle Triassic. Remember this stage of the floating continents?"

"Yes!" the little animals cheered together.

"Well done! Gradually the climate changed from dry to humid. At the end of the period, a major mass extinction occurred that gave way to dinosaurs in the Jurassic Period."

LYSTROSAURUS, LAND VERTEBRATE

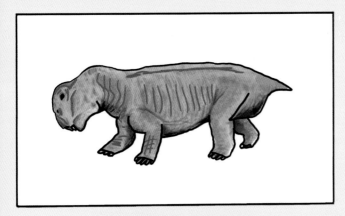

ONE OF THE FIRST DINOSAURS COELOPHYSIS

PROTEROSUCHUS, A CROCODILE LIKE REPTILE

SELLOSAURUS PLATEOSAURUS AN EARLY PROSAUROPOD

CYNOGNATHUS A MAMMAL LIKE ANIMAL

"In the Jurassic Period, the Age of Reptiles, there were small extinctions at the end and beginning. The two land masses, Laurasia and Gondwana, drifted forming the ocean Tethys in the middle. The dry climate gave way to a humid climate. The fauna was dominated by dinosaurs. The first birds appeared. The first placental mammals appeared. Early lizards appeared. There were marine and land dinosaurs. Pterosaurs were the dominant flying vertebrates," Owl continued to explain.

MURAENOSAURUS, A SEA DINOSAUR

DIPLODOCUS, A LAND DINOSAUR

CONIFERS WERE DOMINANT IN JURASSIC, DOUGLAS FIR

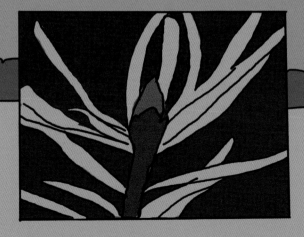

"The Cretaceous Period spanned 79 million years. It was warm and saw many inland seas populated by animals no longer living today. Dinosaurs dominated the land. New groups of birds, mammals, and flowering plants appeared. The period ended with a large mass extinction of animals ushering in the Cenozoic Era." As Owl said this he smiled, thinking of his early ancestors.

CYLOSAURUS A FIERCE SEA DINOSAUR

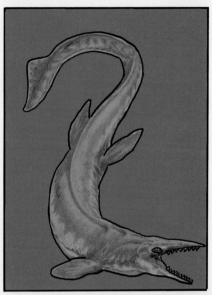

TYRANNOSAURUS REX A LAND DINOSAUR

PLETOSAURUS, A FLYING REPTILE

"Lasting from 66 ma to 23 ma, Paleogene saw the spread of mammals and birds and the dying of deep sea plants due to climate change. Mammals inhabited the seas and grew to be whales. They also inhabited land and grew to be elephants. On land they became lions and small animals like gophers. They also became big animals like bears. Just like you'll be one day, little cub!" Owl said ruffling his fur.

The cub smiled and asked, "What about goslings?"

Owl turned to the little gosling and said, "On trees they grew to be primates paving way to the appearance of humans. And birds took to the skies and grew to be eagles, hawks, chickadees, and geese. Just like you'll be one day, little gosling. As the Earth cooled, hot, temperate, and cold climates came into existence. Flora and fauna responded by adapting and evolving to be different species."

TYPICAL MID-PALEOGENE SCENE FLORA AND FAUNA

Owl went on. "The Neogene Period is notable for further development of mammals and especially humans. North America and South America joined, cutting off the Pacific from the Atlantic. This created the Gulf Stream, changing the climate and producing changes in flora and fauna. The cooling culminated in the glaciations in the Quaternary Period."

"This is a brief 600 million year history of life - of Cambrian Trilobites, Ordovician Graptolites, Silurian Fish, Devonian Forests, Carboniferous Amphibians, Permian Proliferations, Triassic Diversification, Jurassic Reptiles, Cretaceous Dinosaurs, and early mammals, birds, and flowering plants, Paleogene mammals, Neogene primates, and Quaternary humans. These were a series of massive extinctions followed by newer and more suited animals," concluded Owl.

"Thank you for telling us this fascinating story," said the gosling and the cub.

"You are welcome. Now let me sleep," said Owl closing his eyes.

About the Author

Holding an M.Sc. in Geophysics from the Osmania University in Hyderabad, Tel, India and a Ph.D. in Physics from the University of Alberta, Edmonton, AB, Canada, Dr. N. Naveen Chandra taught at Universities in India, Canada, Brazil, and Mozambique. He also worked as a Geologist and Geophysicist for over thirty years, contributing scientific papers to journals and conferences. He taught Mathematics, Physics, Computer Science, and Special Education for over fifteen years at York Region District School Board and Toronto District School Board. In 2014, Naveen authored *Big Bang as Told by Owl, Floating Continents as Told by Owl,* and a Polar Graph of Elements which can be found at UCLA data base http://www.meta-synthesis.com/webbook/35_pt/pt_database.php?PT_id=661. He made presentations at schools on the use of the new Polar Graph as a teaching tool and resource material. Naveen became a member of the American Chemical Society on invitation and can be reached at chandraalex@hotmail.com.